Flying Inland

Flying Inland

KATHLEEN SPIVACK

Doubleday & Company, Inc.
Garden City, New York
1973

Some of these poems first appeared in publications: MYTHMAKING, in *Poetry*, Copyright © 1966 by Modern Poetry Association, HIGH, *Poetry*, Copyright © 1968 by Modern Poetry Association, NIGHT TERROR, THE WATER GIVES UP ITS COUNSEL and DRIFTING, *Poetry*, Copyright © 1969 by Modern Poetry Association, THE TANK, THE SNAPPING TURTLE, *Poetry*, Copyright © 1970 by Modern Poetry Associaton, RAIN, *Poetry*, Copyright © 1971 by Modern Poetry Association, and DIDO: SWARMING, *Poetry*, Copyright © 1972 by Modern Poetry Association; STRAINING, METAMORPHOSIS, NERVED UP, DEDALUS, BLURRING, LOBOTOMY and FAT-LIPPED, YOU FORMLESS, *Atlantic Monthly*; NOW THE SLOW CREATION, *Harper's Magazine*, Copyright © 1973 by the Minneapolis Star and Tribune Company, Inc., and EATING, *Harper's Magazine*, BUT YOU, MY DARLING, *Antioch Review*, Copyright © 1970 by Antioch Review Incorporated; FLYING INLAND, *Boston After Dark*; THE EMBRYO, PRIVATE PAIN IN TIME OF TROUBLE and A CHILD'S VISIT TO THE BIOLOGY LAB, *Antaeus*, Copyright © 1973 by Antaeus; ORPHANS, *Ms.*, Copyright © 1973 by Ms. Magazine Corp.; the poem MARCH 1st appeared originally in *The New Yorker*; THE MAD GIRL WITH SECRET DREAMS, *The Nation*, Copyright © 1973 by the Nation Associates, Inc.; NOT EVEN THE SMALLEST, *Peacefeelers*; VISIONS and I AM, *Sumac*, Copyright © 1969 by Sumac Press; A NURSERY RHYME and EDVARD MUNCH: THE RED-HAIRED GIRL, *Old West Review*, Copyright © 1973 by The Old West Review; THE FLYING DREAM and ICARUS, *Arion's Dolphin*; THE BURGLAR, *The Boston Review*, Copyright © 1968 by The Boston Review; CRIPPLES, *Encounter*, Copyright © 1967 by Encounter Ltd.; THE MEETING, *Women/Poems*, Copyright © 1971 by Women in the Arts; TOADS, *The New England Galaxy*; TO REGENERATE ONESELF, SEPTEMBER: HOME, *Nimrod*, Copyright © 1973 by University of Tulsa.

FOR MY PARENTS

Grateful acknowledgment is made to the Radcliffe
Institute for Independent Study, under whose auspices
this book took final form.

9

I

NOT EVEN THE SMALLEST, THE MOST TENDER

not even the smallest, the most tender
of the animals has forgotten
the small place, the walls
of his touch.

the field mouse remembers
the hole under the piled hay;
always and forever
he will be earth-aching,
smelling the warm manure of spring.

even the shy earthworm
returns. the webbed frog
and all secretly winged
beasts. desire is
like an old onion
at their hearts. they return.
who knows what longings of the mole
go unfulfilled?

Sojourning alone in Paris,
he thought, now finally
he was a poet. All the props
were his: the cloak, the hat
like a cringing accordion,
the mustache, the walking stick
pronouncing ends-of-sentences
on the sidewalk.

Only he had not reckoned
on the loneliness. Isolate,
terrible as a lavatory,
it chilled him, coming in from
the warm purple streets.
His room lay in the darkness
like a terrapin, promising nothing.

Something unseen, a posterity,
crouched in the corners, watching,
ticking off his movements: his forearms
as he washed his shirt
in the basin; the casual
lighting of a match. That eerie tiger
noticed everything. His neck
prickled at his writing stand.

"If you love me, guard
my solitude," he wrote
to endless mistresses, his wife,
his friends. Solitude!
It is the sallow wallpaper
of furnished rooms.
Worried as a snail, he worked,
extruding a thin slimy track.

While to him a young man
earnestly wrote: Dear Mr. Rilke,
how shall I become a poet,
having a most desperate longing
to do so, and in my bosom
some small songs?

And like a garden, the replies
profused, lavishing
in leaking roses, borders
of bachelor's-buttons, blue
at the buttonhole,
and the scent of solitary
sentry lilies: sentences
burgeoning like blood from a slit
artery.

No tourniquet could staunch it.
The heart, spurting, sprinted
onto the page. "Dear Mr. Kappus . . ."
Loneliness, that leech obscene
on his mouth, was sucking,
glutting out whole sonnets,
clots of sound.

Rilke, my river, I know your locked look of a poet:
how from your fingers spun threads
that suspended the universe,
the marionette angels curving and swaying,
sculptural, sermonal bodies.

You sought a shuddering, glorious silence
carved like a crèche; the shriek of a hare, inescapable,
fixing its mute-pooling eyes on a trapper
all hairy and heaving, hunting it down.
Everything holding its breath!

What can follow such terrible silence but salt?
In this ashland, I cup hands
to the Dark River, watch watery lovers,
eyesocketed, flow out of the mind
into a delta of touch.

I see women with blossoming bottoms,
hair like a thicket, flying up from their men
like firebrands, crying angrily "Now, now!"
The men watchful, their pupils dilating,
cougars at night as the brush takes flame.

Crouched under words is a flowering of panthers,
the exquisite jungle, reeking
of vaginal unguents. Green as crushed vine,
slit-eyed boas retwine, palpable,
growing into trees thick as thighs.

At each eyepoint a comet's gone crazy.
Breasts halve in the dark, blossoms
burst their dark nipples. The corners
fill up with bel canto. Camellias
devour the curve of the world—

genitalia unfolding, what secrets!
The brain, in its silence,
grows things behind its eyes.
Like a lily, like fingers, a stubborn root,
visions, narcissi, explode from their bulbs.

BUT YOU, MY DARLING, SHOULD HAVE MARRIED THE PRINCE

When we were children, clasping hands,
do you remember that moist circle, play?
How we were dancing and knew only the dandelions,
and the earth was livid with dandelions.
I see us now as in a photograph that never was:
hair like soapbubbles spun by nuns, the singing
raucous as starch. Our cries still echo
down the corridors of my ears: we,
rank and weedy, wanting to be old.

There were no secrets then
to prickle our knees.
No one hid in the closet.
Beards were friendly as forests of grass—
how we trembled, pretending to be lost,
caught in the chins of uncles.

We pared apples, made wishes,
and washed in the first dew of May.
Mother went through our laundry
and we didn't mind . . .
but how we wept when our cousin got married.
Home from the army, his six-month mustache
saluted both sides of his face.
Jealous as bridesmaids we watched
as he married the girl. She had apricot hair
and a cameo ring.
Look, now, how he takes her hand.
Never was it like that, picking scabs!
Peaches and morning were right for those two,
not for us, little pickles, fevered in bed, yanking
knots from our furious hair in the dark
and begging to be blonde.

Nights came. Net notching our chests,
thighs sticky, we went to the dances
and put up our hair.
You lost your virginity
in mother's garden
and finally I was kissed.

Now we are older. You are married.
Natashas both, we have grown up.
Those shivery wonderings lit from the street
are over; cousins put away in paper boxes.
Outside, the walnut trees
grow sticky as old tears
and I lie sweating in the dark.
The dusk comes swallow-winged;
the apples rot with wishes.
Where there is no magic, one stays a toad
and we who screamed to know it
know it, and grow old.

It is winter.
I undergo the Death of the Heart,
tramping about in my black fur
coat and boots,
locked into

a small numb circle,
the doors closed, no entry,
mouth and the other pocket shut.
December, you seal me
in ice

keen as a splinter
nailed into the heart.
Absence of feeling
when the thermometer rockets
sub zero.

This stone in my stomach;
this frostbitten
much hoarded Pear:
I assent to its
shriveling.

How I long to be
saved by some Christian
solution: evergreens
warming the snow,
a new birth—

there's a heat—all that
blood steaming
out of an opening,
clotting into a cry to be
reckoned with!

Little Kim, of mixed blood,
adopted, surveyed
his world like a pasha

and found it good.
Conferring delight
like royalty

he received, delighted,
due ecstatic homage.
Pleased, it made him clap his hands.

Losing his life
in his sleep,
he wore a most peeved

expression: how
can it be
that Kim no longer is?

By his death
he silenced an entire sunlit house.
He stilled the dustmotes in the doorways
and expunged
even the footfalls on the floor.

His crib
unceremoniously
removed, his things
were hustled out—"Be quick,"
said death the burglar.

And the mother herself,
rigid and byzantine,
moved stiffly in dark
odoriferous clothes.
We must make do.

Out of the trunks
comes the old grief.

PRIVATE PAIN IN TIME OF TROUBLE

How can I sustain
this troubled swelling:
my heart like an eggplant,

blackened, bulbous, grows too greedy:
bruised and sorrowful
it will not let its great loss go,

wanting to be pendulous with child.
Private pain in time of trouble
as the dark-eyed children burn.

They stretch out their small hands to me:
sparrows, and I do not hear.
It is a false spring this year.

Stirring, straining, toenails, talons gripping
the sheets,
he rounds the next curve: elevation's so
easy!
A wind's huddle, gathering hurdle of birches that's
handled:
he negotiates flight and he's up, the wind tearing
drops from his eyes
and the land passing soberly under.

His shadow, the solemn spread of a man flying, lifts itself
over sprawled hayfields,
looms, purple thought, over water unglistened
by whitecaps,
casts itself over the ocean, flat, introspective,
holding back, holding
back, splayed on the sky, the momentum controlled
as a hawk's, a deliberate celebration

of the simple, his wings streamed back in the praying
position,
his body smiling forward as a ship's prow dividing
the clean air,
no motion, no emotion, only the steady flight
above houses,
the macaw-sun chattering, the burly noises of heaven.

Fatlipped, you formless scavenging
creature, murgling polliwog
munching the algae in my aquarium,
who would believe those skinny legs,
half-formed, would do for a frog?

Some see in that sucking mouth
progress, others a cyclical
moon and a sloughing off.
Tail cloudy as aspic,
tadpole, we dredged you

out with a net from the
cemetery pond. And the seepage
in lowspots, the hollows condensing,
brooding you thick as a root:
is there reason?

Strange how the breeding
goes on in the swamps; fine-legged teeming
in muck and in coffins, weeds
swarming with such events, even
our moist coupling part of it:

all flesh, cookie-dough,
melting, concocting.
Comma, how your large head
bulges, trying and
trying to become a frog!

There is a saying something without words—
this snowfall clotting from a dizzy sky,
a rhythmical intake of breath—and then
no words again.

On our street all the cars are crouching, white.
I woke this morning from a sleep like snow,
as blank and muffling, crying for you to come
and hear me, suffocating, dumb.

You didn't. Now we stand at the front door,
thickened by waking. Groggy snow, no wind,
grows heavily. Thoughts piling as we watch,
our shoulders, fingers touch

but swaddled, absent. Life of your very own,
how can you grow so near, and yet not me?
Five seagulls, circumflex accents, drift by—
nothing to speak of in the heaving sky.

II

Now the slow creation of things
comes everywhere:
the warm lapping of petals
in the sun; the leaf that turns
its sticky surface to the air.

Slowly, my pocket opens like an orange,
warm to your touch;
and that five-petaled sun
folds all its fruited segments out.
I turn forever on that bed.

And out of that arc, delicately rising,
children swim like fish
or seahorses; thistle-slim,
their bellies bent,
into the new-rinsed light.

Who put them there, you put
them there, marvelously fat-fingered.
A great soft whoosh of the breath—
they come, endlessly spinning
like soapbubbles through a pipe.

I have turned into a weasel,
with a weasel's green peeled heart,
a black whorled nose like a thumbprint.

My underbelly's long and sleek
and I've great strength. I love
to stretch and lick my furry length.

You left me in the woods all winter;
I wept cold snot-nosed tears. But strange
how quickly winter disappears.

Eyes nosing into everything,
with paddy paws I lounge among the leaves.
I have forgotten how a human grieves.

Stiff in a white coat,
dragged there by my mother,
I sulked through the laboratory
offices, the halls, the brass
cases, more gloomy than second grade.
My important tummy
strained in its white buttons, fingers
picked at things, sour and impatient as eyes.

Down the hall, the light was fine
as filtered lymph. The sodden chicks,
the unborn piglets swimming in their tears,
went round and round in jars;
the afternoon grew circular.

And babies too. Brine-flowers, their blind eyes
enclosed all specimens of coral.
Where their belly buttons grew
they floated, pink and new as toes.
They swam in a shield of arms.

I thought, that's where the changelings go;
prisoned forever, weeping, waiting for parents,
their arms upflung against knowing.
They have no souls, my mother said.
But I, whose seven years swelled in my eyes,
oh alter ego, fluttered at the glass.

Somewhere the staring cells went wild;
the goggling world grew ripe too fast.
My name, that finger on the yeast, emerged
and swelling now, was swallowed inward.
It was water on the brain.

Crouched like a worm, or incubus, I shouldered
all that dazzling pressure in my arms.
Great shudders shook the growing of my head;
bug-eyed, I watched myself grow slowly dead.

Now twenty-five years later in that brain
the convoluted child unfolds
neat as a cucumber curled in a jar.
Jeweled, hydrocephalic, once again
the pickled images flare in the glass
like snowflakes, struck to rain.

There is in me the sound as of great singing,
the road running like a ribbon, romantic
as a movie screen; sunsets
stretching, vistavision, over the green fields.

And all this scenery is stirring, stirring—
the ending of a Russian film—clasping
hands like clams, while the music
edges, a great Niagara Falls, over "The End . . ."

and the soldier has paid with his blood—
transfusing the Russian army—and the heroine
has become a nurse. Great causes
wiggle, oil-slick on my puddled brain.

Who, too, would not surge from his seat
crying "yes, yes, Patriotism!" and have a purpose
like a clumsy bee, woolly, thick-winged,
bundled up in his furry uniform?

Look! Even now he quivers with his humming,
bumbling with a dull blind passion
(one sting: he stabs and stiffens)
in his cupola of flowers.

A NURSERY RHYME

There were some monkeys who
were taken from their mothers, bred
by a surrogate whose breasts were cotton
and whose head

was chicken wire.
From great falsies flowed the milk,
and those monkeys sucked and sniveled,
clinging to the hulk.

Their wise eyes grew brighter,
cheated. Shriveling, they grew wild as fire.
To eat the surrogate alone became
each one's desire.

Now in their cages
monkeys sit. And monkeys pick, and monkeys do . . .
Each, crouching, shuns the others, dreams
of what he never knew.

One is
what one eats;
we are the pieces
of our parts. So eat
the flannel ears
of eggplants,
chicken hearts.

Pieces of another
form our eye,
our bone, our
skin. The cells
remove and die
and the foreign
ones begin.

The slaughtered meat
lies down in mounds
for us; the great
pigs groan. Cows
in the stock-
yards for our
appetites atone.

So do the carrots.
Wrested from
the dark ground
by their tails, they
twist and thicken.
All their
growing fails

on thick cracked
china plates,
forked fatly,
put to mouth. We

gulp; engorged
the carrots quicken
and swim south.

Out on the prairie,
as we gobble
all the beasts are
eating hay—their
munching faces
patient as they
face one way—

Portable digestive
systems; head to
hay and tail
to wind: in gardens
vegetables strain
and labor. May this
eating never end.

I raced the morning;
at the zenith, turned
to wait.

the sun stood dawdling by his mirror,
the ocean.
faraway the horizon.

hurry up, I cried
and, flying faster,
skimmed the curve of the world

so ran into him from behind.
stay, hold back the sky!
he the heat and I the wind
(never the horizon).

falling, I
have seen the bittern's cry
spiraling upward
behind my eyelids.

What does it mean to be human:
running in a field, the eyes slits,
the face contorted
like the jaw of a jackal?

Terror and fearful pursuit:
babies like bundles
are clutched to the thin chest,
all clawed and huddled,

howling,
hooding the head against horror. Human!

WAR AND THE WATERCRESS GARDEN

Morning, you grainy crust of bread,
I bite my name in you two inches deep.
I am always
putting my name on things—
that garden of watercress during the war
with K.R.D. standing out in green.
The planes droning overhead were warned:
let K.R.D. alone!

Green in my lunchbox, green in my sandwiches,
watercress watered every morning
toted like anyone's name to school.
On my mother's belly she tattooed me,
growing huge as a circus balloon.
Kathleen Romola Drucker;
the letters stretched. Birth!
Somebody knew who I was.

So from my wizened thumb-in-water
I identify myself. Thumbs in paint.
Thumbs in the garden out with father
fussing with tomato plants.
I squat and watch
my folks pick off tomato worms;
their horny jaws, their sludgy
yellow blood, eating, eating.

You wrinkled insatiable creatures,
get out of our garden, I shriek.
My kinsmen, German accidents,
implacably snatched at
by worms and such
while I, Vermonter, newly come,
try to blackout my German
tongue, speak English now

with mother, in the hopeful sun
among the bean poles
and cucumber.
Mother, you gave me
a plot of my own in father's field;
that watercress garden
laid out in initials,
keeping the planes off,
staking my claim.

My son, striving Icarus, lovesick
unendingly, sweating, forlorn
with a voice that blats
suddenly, flawed like the horn

of a blatant new model,
your eyes hold the glare
of brash lamps, far too raw
for the delicate sharpshooter air

that you, too, want to dare.
Do you hope to achieve there a cure
for that acne, calm for knock-
knees, a wingsbreadth secure-

ing your future, painting the sky
with a stammering streamer of words
ordered like literature?
Don't pretend you're a bird;

leave the ego to me!
Shield your eyes from the sun
and stick home with your mother,
your chin furred with crumbs

in the sprawl of her apron,
nestling and croaking. Watch on TV
how I work with contraptions
to outwit my weight. Systematically

concentrating, I've derived a
balance, through certain regimes,
that lightens my body, thoughts
that surpass even mechanical means

and my mind, so encouraged,
now strains to glimpse god.
Work at your visions at
home, boy, while you applaud

your Old Man at his business, willed
airward by nerve. When you've found
control easy you'll earn the large curve:
the arc of the eagle must be deserved.

Sadness, sadness. A room
darkened by sadness.
At night, alone,
standing, wringing my hands,

my eyes are fugitives
from the circle of light
and dusk, like a warning, settles down
to the echoing smells

of a house left empty, aloof
from the feathery
odor of food; no stew
sticking to saucepan,

no crisp acrid crust
to cling under cold water.
The pans are empty, tin
in the sink, the utensils

unused. And a faucet's
been dripping all day,
wearing away a brown track:
the rust of its life

searing and spoiling;
the sediment staining
the whiteness like thought.
Think of the trickling

going on all alone
when the walls are as empty
as fists, when the windows, amnesia,
look out and forget,

when the furniture,
freed from the imprint of bodies,
marshals itself like parents deserted.
Think of the dust

that deceives, insisting while
all's seeming empty: the convolution
muffled, gathering like a horror:
oh brain, too much marked cave!

In the halls, in the universities,
the wheel chairs do their slow dance
between classes. Painful caryatids,
they propel themselves down the halls
like enormous maimed grasshoppers.

Last summer, in glaring July,
I stepped on a grasshopper
on a path. It was grasshopper season.
The hay hummed with them and they twitched
like little green twigs in the sun.

Under my foot, the insect
was only partially crushed.
Almond-eyed and slow, he tried
to drag his soft parts, severed legs
onto the side of the path;

the reproach of the crippled.
Now far from summer, lying in bed,
I think, oh body, how I love you.
Moving so easily, may no harm come to you;
long bones, legs, hands up to light.

Susan, we meet in late fall
in the bitter wind.
But while I in my blue cape
grieve for my dead baby, you grow
in your purple cape a huddled
hidden living child.

And I am reminded
of the meeting of Mary
and Elizabeth, the mothers
of Jesus and John the Baptist,
with the Giotto hills rising, steep humps,
in the background. Each woman
has placed her hand
on the abdomen of the other: within each
a child leaps.

It is fall, perhaps November there.
For each, the birth date nears.
The skies are grey, though the Italian
hills break from shadow.
Their draperies glow;
Mary, of course,
in blue. And Eliza-

beth. What sweetness,
such a meeting of women!
Brief respite from the bitterness
of winter: they do not suspect
the suffering to follow.
It is said
the two children spoke to each other,
then, from within their wombs.

Now, standing on the flagstones
in our capes whose shapes
are gothic windows, we
are silent: deprivation
chokes me in the cold; you have
such secrets; you are
heavy with hope.

And as the snow flakes, salt
flakes fall, the world
grows large and vacant: I think
of those pale women, leaning inward,
and of how
their small sons, unborn John and Jesus,
recognized each other
and kicked
their mothers with joy and
evangelical fervor.

III

Coming out of the house on a fresh March morning,
I saw February still meandering around
like laundry, caught in a Bendix. Stray shreds
of cloud, like pillowslips, were rent from
her large endlessness. Outdated,
her decrepit body garlanded itself dis-
gracefully with powder. She luxuriated in old age.
Even her greying sheets were still there,
tattered, heaped carelessly on the street,
bearing the indentation of someone's huge body
and furred with a fine fringe of soot.
She had been plump, she had been heavy, sitting
on top of us since January. Winter, you
old clothes hamper, what mildew
still molders inside you before March
dribbles a bit, dries up, and is done for?

In the hall, scuffling; in the cat's mouth, a dove.
Oh startled exclamations! The bird is cooing soft
excitable alarms. You, plural, wake
at odds, from fuzzy dreams and
thick-with-hashish mating, disentangling
the white flannel nightgown
from the legs that struggle
for firm ground; wrenched
by cries from the maw of bed
to the gaping mouth of the entry.

A dove! The cat is casual, smiling:
he will not be dispossessed.
You've had your fun of his fur
body, stuffed with marijuana,
brain, the target, blurring
to a small determined rage. He's earned
the things he gets between his jaws;
the crunchy bird bones, knowledge, and the white
wood-smooth body.

Look how I suffer, beckons now the bird.
I who have dared
investigate the air, who've found
clear weather at the rim.
I have hallucinated land
as crisp as light.
My flicker-yellow eye has unreeled sky:
now I am forced to watch
my homecoming, the draggle-tail
in hall, the sacrificial feast

where you sit down at table,
cracking the joints of the girl
in your teeth
and she gets her revenge
by going limp and refusing;
her impenetrable
feathers blurring your pleasure, tucked in
the subtle white grimace of bed.

Hurried into a box, the dove,
back of the stove, pants
and recovers. Blood on her feathers
and soot like a slick on them, glassy
and evil. A chuck of her head
and the quick breathing
slackens: her breast heaves with
gossip; the eye shuts,
reliving. You are sickened

in retrospect, feeling again
the curved bird in the mouth,
the blood hardened like rind
and the terror that tore through
your feigned-passion fucking
and woke you from sex
like the shriek of a child.

From where did it come? The world flounders
in water; the household submerges in sleep.
The bird's bedded
and nests by your side,
a small feathery hump.
In the cave of the nightgown
perhaps you will grope for
each other's warm parts again.
What else, my potheads,
high, indefatigable,
would you be doing
with a dove in your place?

Some moral decisions
one is incapable of making.
Perhaps all.

The child within
was bleeding. Done for.
Something at the worst

gone wrong. Paralyzed,
incapable, I pursued
the term unmoving

while to walk the stairs
would finish off
the creature. But

how can one? When one wants so—
yet one feels it, inside,
struggling? There are conflicts

human beings can only hold to
by a sort of shutting off.
At the center,

irrevocable as failure,
the child thrashed, making
its final move.

I am the ruined queen:
imperious, go down, go down.
I cling to trees till the black
clotted bodies open me,

and one thick circle. Swarm in the air.
The rich round honey jar
is empty now. The husk sloughs off.
I go where no bees are.

Sting one last time! They say
stabbed swans disguise their throats
with song. How inadvised
to choke on the first note,

buzzing in misery, to vibrate
in the throng like any fly.
Remind me I am queen
and warm me while I die

wrapped in my stiffened wings:
I should have had the globe!
Vein in the rigid wrist instead;
I harden like a scab.

EDVARD MUNCH: THE RED-HAIRED GIRL

A red-haired girl stands in the street.
A red-haired vine crawls up her thigh.
Where is it climbing?
Lifesblood, vein like a twining tree,
it shall suck her empty.
It shall embrace her like a man,
hissing such secrets,
insidious, that her insides
shall liquefy, flowing out, oh

in the dark. Yes, it shall insist
till her milk-thigh trembles
till her knee
wobbles till her leg
gives way in its lax curve:
till the dark river runs down.
And the vine shall plant small fingers on her groin,
tentative at first,
at first its gentle pressure like a tickle
as she eases toward it;
then, gripping her softest parts, ever growing,
and she with her full weight
hanging soft toward the belly,
rooting more firmly.
She sucks in air
and the fingers nail inward.

Flesh conquered. The vine sends out rivulets.
Each rivulet's a red strand.
Each strand's a flame.
Groping, the growing thinks, where next?
Upward, of course. She's frozen to the spot.
A tongue a tentacle
to her secret parts.

Oh look! The flames are eating her up. See on the street
a red-haired girl
with greenish bruises on her flesh
while the hair on her scalp begins to jump and dance
to join the festivities.
It sends out spasms. It straightens itself.
It curls and jerks;
it stretches yearningly toward her breasts.
Twining around her neck
where the small bird pulses,
thinking of strangling, it chooses against it
in favor of tasting more.

Twitching like a mad thing
it creeps hurriedly down. It's a caress, all right;
an itch that drives one wild:
the vine secretly extending,
the hair menacing, withholding,
all parts of her body discovered,
choked off.
See on the street a girl consumed by poison:
see how her mouth is wet.
Soon she shall flare like a lamp,
her hands, her semaphores, all crimson.

In the steel harbor
the slate grey flakes are falling,
plushing onto the tourmaline water;
a dusk of concrete.
The sky is salmon-hushed
and slow: my ship
breathes on the water
like a flat grey lung.

All's watercolored, wet.
The boat pulls out,
reflective, panting. Wharves
seep off behind.
A horn brays, shuddering:
the sun a smallpox
vaccination on the sky.

A heavy rhythm in the hold.
Blood at the throat beats warningly:
I'm leaving something, leaving.
The crowd retreats
at the pier,
seedlings cast out
by our departure.

Oh dirty city, lump of coal,
you held my fevers
smothered in a flower,
ash-enclosed, too long.
It's all gone
up the chimney now; one flash,
a flare of soot.

Light up a skyline
of thermometers! The ship
swings round behind
this glitter-eyed, greying
evening, tubercular.
I am too sensible to cry.
Good-by, good-by.
Squat England huddles
on the other side.

To regenerate oneself
as the tree toad, chameleon, the tail-wick
does; no, that's not easy to do.

Regrowing the appendage, the tail that was missing,
sometimes in haste sprouting two: I could be
a glass lizard, tweaking and skittering

with the very thing wanted, unselfpitying:
a creature of crepe toes,
gripping the tree with a whistle of triumph.

THE JUDGMENT

In the blurring low-blood-pressure
center of the night,
needle choked at zero, clothes
like strangled bodies on the chairs,
struggling awake—oh, oh, oh—vomiting!

Stumbling in the john before the pitiless
toilet and a wild-eyed light, who is
this splay-foot murderous monster
churning out of me? Mouths everywhere, on
all unnatural parts, what poisons

can a body hold? Crouched on the plaid
linoleum, my body sacrifices more.
The glittering machinery of plumbing
eases it away. In my sick odor
is a victim's gratitude.

Standing at the bathroom door
you worry that I am "all right." Don't
look! Your little one, amazed, is
slobbering evil, retching, gagging. Shut
the door to your heart and gut!

Your wide white face can scarcely register
these pink grotesqueries pouring out—
tomatoes, supper, unknown matters racing
to reveal themselves. So brave, love,
in the face of unbearable truths? And now

it's over. I am docile. I've confessed.
Run all the taps! Clean sheets, clean
nightgown: to be crucified and then
led to such whiteness in the end!
You stroke my hair till dawn sears us,
clear, trembling, tart as fresh pineapple.

NURSING GRIEF IN THE EARLY MORNING

I am divided because you are free;
and trapped most terribly: being vulnerable.

Shouting from a nightmare
where these thoughts are nesting in my brain,
the words will out, enormous
printed letters, in our bedroom,
dank with sleep at dawn.
For while I dream of children
you sleep on, oblivious and calm.

And I, who still hang on, have been betrayed
by how quickly your recovery's made.

"Quick, quick, she's washing herself!"
Four nurses like nightbirds hurriedly gather,
framed in my door.
"What a good girl!"

I am again like a little child
woken up from a night dream of sickness;
tousled, tussling with darkness,
flushed: who are those bright strangers?

They have set a basin of warm water before me.
Soap, too, and towels of a whiteness.
Heavy, the sheet with its cool weight:
I lean up on one elbow.

Can it really be water, with its pure ripple?
Water, the warm drops catching a radiance?
Such wetness waking me from a night blank on the brain:
water, with its green shine?

I am innocent as any creature
dabbling, becoming clean.
"Look, she's washing herself!"
I feel myself to be indeed obedient and good.

I dangle hamburg on a pencil end:
your huge jaws go for it, hinged.
Clawfoot, I see you devouring
whole bodies, legs eaten down
to the knee, engaging your gut
while the arms, the hair streaming,
cannot help but succumb.
Under your carapace
all things become carrion.

We toss you gobbets of girls.
In the fishfood fall the shapes
of shaved women, twisted, imploring.
Cheers for the sacrifice! But still
the dull belly desires: writhing limbs
cannot cure you; nothing can ease
this determined stupidity,

snapping, insensate,
missing the fatty mass, bumping,
bewildered, against the scummed glass.
Can it be that you eat without rancor?
Ancient, armored, chomping blindly, your shell
harbors slime like an emblem of greed.

They are bringing over a shipment
of Vietnamese war orphans—
my friend tells me—do you want one?
We walk up the hill, our hearts clunking.

Those ink-black eyes
unblinking as a creature's,
the thin splayed fingers
holding on—to supply
for the tree frog
its grip on the bark . . .

In Korea, when a lady
doctor visited the orphanages,
flocks of blackbird children circled, piping
words she couldn't decode.
Then at last, resolved the accent,
she could hear them clearly, pleading,
"Please. Please. Buy. Home. Me."

They have walled in the frog:
beating and beating till his green heart
would burst, he broke himself
against the cellar wall.

Under a house eight stories high
this beast, who cannot cry,
weeps tears of chalk. That live tree, anguish,
forces its way through stone.

No one hears me hammering on pillows
in the dark. Nor sweating,
squat in my own chest,
you frog, my brother.

A droning silence grows in me;
my eyes are milky, though I see.
And everywhere a nervous doom
moves like a woman in the room.

Cradling myself, I rock and turn
to see my reckless family burn
to its bare elements; before long
we shall lie netted in our wrongs,

hauled up like herring on the beach,
our windy city out of reach;
white-bellied, gasping, turning blue—
first to fish-eye, and then to glue.

Sound without speech, speech without sound,
do fishes weep when they are found?
Oh, men of Troy, give back the girl:
the glob in the throat, the fisher's pearl.

The hot sun on toads
and the gold eye slitting leisurely.
In the woods the warm earth
gives off its dark smell
comforting as ordure.

If I could catch for one moment
the massive renunciation of the creatures,
hunched, silent, splay-footed,
their wrinkled skins cool
under the onslaught.

Such gaiety of heat does not perturb them:
no dizzy ecstasy, head reeling, the toes
gripping harder; their patient
long-term adoring can wait:
they are in reserve.

Toads, in your small hearts
is there not some longing?
A ruby grabbyness, fierce and cold?
The sap rises, the water shimmers, the woods thrash joyously:
you hold yourselves stone-still as for the second coming.

I am
Leonardo, endlessly sublimating,
the sex bleeding out
in fine scribbles of ink.
Freud, his jaw rotting, helpfully blundering,
turning friends on to cocaine by mistake,
painfully searching
while patients in droves lined up
for forgiveness-diplomas;
he saw and was humble:
I am he, in his earnestness, his jealousies.

Joyce in his slimfingered blindness
hungered for family, knew himself failing.
Frost, too, the old slyboots, avoided defining:
while misfortune nailed down each icicle
he misled the critics. And went on writing.
Nietzsche, lonely, muttering, mad
on your mountain, what rye mash
of history are you creating?
And Sado and Maso, that impossible
marriage, glued belly to belly
under my skin?

In the light of ovens
grate-bones burn. And I, too, stoke the fires,
suck the marrow, can't escape
this century, this drowning Frisian island where
the fish eat ruined libraries
and cannot learn.

IV

Beauty is never satisfied
with beauty. Helen,
gazing in the glass,
framed by the lecherous curtains,
the enchanted bed,
knew herself beautiful. Yet she felt life pass
about her. Laughter had been hers
to breed alone. Now mute,
the humdrum pulse run down, she lay
a palpitation of her memory;
a deceitful body and a crumbling smile
were all that love and elixirs had bred.

Men knew her aging odor.
Ravished by the nosings of her fears,
she married. Her fastened gaiety became a jewel
decking a sot. Oh well, we do
with what we have and haven't got;
the pagan cried
against endurance, dressed
and went to dinner at the side
of Menelaus. What would she become, if not her men
would come inside her,
make her whole again!
Each night was Helen
on the reminiscent bed
waiting with spread heart and legs
and willing arch for willing arrowhead.

Sprung from the cracking bow of Troy
he could not notice Helen growing old,
but fitted as a flower, or a toy,
as use to pleasure, went to hold
the woman in his arms.

And were they satisfied, these two,
when afterwards Helen closed her eyes
and slept?
Helen, who turned the too-much heart
to a great dumb shriveling, could do as much
to any lover.
So squandered Paris in her arms lay dry
and she lay lavish and methodical;
(who offers bread by night may offer mold)
beauty to beauty did not satisfy;
such meetings of perfections cut us, turn us cold
as aging Helen, bittering in her sleep,
and cheat us of desire
by too much hungering.

She must have been glad to wake, not to be satisfied,
to see her husband stir himself and raise a fleet,
and all the world fall shadow
to the crumpling of that sheet.

THE TANK

They are like convicts in the pen,
the grey forms shaping, tail to fin,
a movement that's a habit. Ominous and eating,
nothing survives their quest for more.
We planted vegetation: it was eaten.
Swamp grass. Algae. Bitten to the quick
till our attempts subsided.
Hunks of rock. The circling fish

take exercise, the big ones—mind
your distance—prowling
on the littler. Sometimes insurrection
flares: a snarling flash, a darting eye,
a sudden snatch at a fin
as quickly quelled. Stark, monotone,
the barren tank, the green all eaten,
bleeds them grey.

Oh diversion, let us have a death!
The bigger the better.
Something to make our Sundays
meaningful, while grey as newsprint,
as the Sunday paper, time sifts up
and chokes us in imprisonment. Throw us
a fish found belly-first one morning,
dead from bullying:

a whitened, eyes-up blimp that bloats
in silence on the murk until our bravest,
Mouth-to-the-Ears, ventures a jagged bite. At last
there's blood in the water! All can eat!
The browny grains of fluid ooze. Raw, ravening,
the flesh in strings hangs from their jaws:
the pleading corpse submissive now.
Fish in a ring. Lockstep. Chainstep.

Griddle, licking her tits
till the milk came hard,
laid her soft belly out to our gaze
while she stiffened;
then as the pinker grew spotted
and dark,
she spawned six wet kittens.
We envied, amazed.

Oh to have kittens,
small things with fur
on them, popping in unison
into the world,
nudging and urging the water-white
stuff from you
with their toes, scratching and
gratified, curled.

Helpless, near-hairless, their fetal form
drives them still,
urgent blunt snouts that
sniff milk and go wild;
and Griddle lies meekly and
mawkishly watches:
she purrs with the smugness
of woman with child.

Blind persistence wins out in this
game of surviv-
al. Fresh from wet waking, quite
frantic with greed,
they drag at her nipples,
leaking, hung longer,
and can't be distracted from
keeping alive.

My brains were large silver coins in a piggy bank:
someone had dropped them in through the slot;
had painted pink roses on my back
and put a curl in my tail.
My eyes shone with a flat ceramic glaze.

And as I turned slowly on a table,
the room swam dully off my surface
and the money jingled and clinked.
I was a stoutly magnificent pig:
my own porcelain prisoner.

At night the money rattled frantically.
Nowhere to spend it, and no one to spend.
It multiplied so fast there was almost
no room for it. I was one pig
who was thinking furiously.

How I longed for someone to release me,
smashing, finding in the shards
huge wheels of silver, half dollars and dimes,
the money crying, chink chink.
But no one would commit this destruction.

A few more coins could still be fitted in;
by now I had the habit of thought.
Greedy so long and so hoarding,
my eyes bulged with the pressure
and my adenoids enlarged.

So I shall always love you, my liberator,
who found me straining, flushed
beneath my flowers. For you,
with infinite patience and a bent
hairpin, have relieved me.

Women and men:
bend, bend.
I lie beside you
till our lives like offshoots end.

As morning stirs, a greyness
draws us to the other's heart,
and our ribs, rubbing, comfort
though our griefs howl, caged apart.

The pressure of your bones
insisting against mine,
face against warm hair: how breathy, how
ineffable to have you there

when lovely, locked together
softly, you are berth and bed
and respite from
what lies ahead.

Better there be no house, than always the stringing
of these bones.
Such an encumbered marriage: crated with
knickknacks and negligees
to keep us trying; the chirping furniture
a herd which drags my carcass
through the living room by day,
and I so malcontent, why do I stay
to verify a house, a job,
my edifice of disillusionment?

The body, as decay, gives off its heat. I sit
among the wreckage that surrounds my kind,
casting the wreckage off behind
and trail myself. Daily, wives grow more unkind
and pink, and I must do with what was done
when glutton, be content
with television—plastic tit—
count calories while they invent
a better kind of missile kit.

But oh, it was not always like this:
such a sky when we came to this place
on the beach in november—was it november?
Times we were songless and lithely alone,
oh how lovely, that petrified garden.
How we came dripping with ocean and laughter
and salty as seafish, as starlight,
and naked, the love began.

White leaves, hands, lay light on our loving,
bruised us black as desire; they stumbled us shoreward.
We are not like the others, we cried;
and running away, we returned.
How well now we have learned
indifference. Better to have died.

Too late, old love, come summer soon again
we would not know it from this hunched
hen-pinching warmth. The ospreys will not mate
inside our house. The sea birds die.
How long must I scratch in this racketing bed
for curio memories? I catch at the dial
and the screen of my head
blurs me dead.
I am stuffed for a chair.

All my life to forget—
and you, love, cosmetically young as a daughter—
how somewhere the uncluttered bones are salty and lie still,
and how happy the green weeds in water.

Behold the chimp
in solitary confinement:
every day he must undergo
catcalls and jeers

For the edification of small children
whose hands thrust peanuts
at his bulk, to take pleasure
in seeing him refuse them.

Beleaguered, he paces his bare white-
lit cell, furrowed and searching
for what next to do.
Sometimes he tries sitting down,

Patiently turning his back to the crowd,
hunching his shoulders, hands
clasping his ankles,
rocking, and to himself,

Whispering the twenty-third psalm.
Or, hour long, he waits by the door
of the hole, the dark cave
he's allowed when the people go home,

Knowing it's locked. No way out!
No corner to eat or to
sleep in; no place to wake slowly
from dreams in which trees figure heavily.

Privacy: what is that?
Does a chimp have the right to privacy?
Does he not defecate like other animals
on concrete while the Keeper watches?

And though his eyes, pinpoints
of canny comprehension, show
he suffers; though he misses, daily,
not one small humiliation,

Politely, he has finally surrendered
"freedom," indeed, can't
survive in it: caged, an anomaly,
baffled, respectable.

THE MAD GIRL WITH SECRET DREAMS

Fat girl from Montana, odd duck,
pressing your face to the flatland
you wrote "I am an unusual person, a genius
in fact." A genius in freckles!
Feet rooted in sagebrush, sullen calves;
they say you were mad
and suffered from an excess of feeling.

Geniuses always identify themselves,
eating, aching, through three meals a day.
What bothered you was your virginity
lying like a stubborn oyster
inland where the sun dries up the dust.
If you could find a focus for your outpourings—
how you longed to be pried open!

Hating being at home, your blunt
jaw like a sawed-off shotgun
held its sight to the mesa
brown as linoleum under the sun,
no target, no distinguishing marks.
Mary MacLane, scrubbing your mother's kitchen
floor, mad young lady, itchy finger,
let your mind go like a dark incendiary.

I am like some soft animal in the night,
fumbling at the latches of a mind
which will not let me enter.
Squatting alone in the dark
I keep patiently twiddling the knobs,
seeking the right combination.

I've fiddled with kaleidoscopes before,
with things that work. They've all
some gimmick, trick. There is a reason
that the egg drops in the bottle
and the wineglass rings. Ali Baba, too,
had patience in the cave.

Around me, five o'clocks fall down
like pears. Squashed morning salivates,
relentless, lumbering. It will not wait.
My muffled hands grow huge. Oh furry beast,
give up, for night has gone; and with it
all the loot. I'm overdrawn.

Sometimes when evening comes and everyone
retires into houses;
and cars crawl home like corridors
of lights, and the sky loses
substance; while husbands and their wives
sit hunched immobile over supper
as puddles harden on the plates:
despair, night terror, reigns.

Then children cry and cannot
put their blocks together,
and quarrels break out: do not let me be alone!
I cannot organize the random world
nor freeze a sensibility
from fragments of blue dusk. Nor, blurring vision,
build a tower in the mind
not baffled by the wind.

And driving home from work
I watch the city turn on,
blink by blink. Each sharky shape's a car,
a sideswiper. Each form's a man.
Each shadow bears a scar, a gun,
a promise; wears its isolation
bandaged by an overcoat. I turn
the wheel. We learn reality by rote.

Two cattle wake in the barn;
two loaves in the oven.
Buttock to comfortable buttock
and the warm flesh rising.

Autumn's returned. We breathe in unison
now in our envelope-bed. Seven years
ruminating, turning life
to the heavy odor of milk

so tender and rich it froths
in the bucket. All the stray cats in town
line up to be fed. It comes creamy
and spurting: plenty of milk!

The air's gold in our stalls:
the munch munch of digestion,
the sighs of two animals feeding
on slow private thoughts

flank against flank. My husband,
no longer my stranger, love is a
substance large as a mother:
we moo together, lowing softly,
stirring awake this fine Sunday morning.

THE WATER GIVES UP ITS COUNSEL

Looking into the water,
stay, oh ripples, just so:
the water widening and widening
and the small thought transitory.

The pure curve of the current:
flow with it, my simple self, flow
with the call of its curling
forever. Recover. Forgo

the sharp sadness.
How we grasp, though we wish it not so!
Will is nothing to water. Time
to learn to let go.

To live in
myself,

not thinking about.

Taking a canoe,
two girls,

down the river

with the blur of autumn
in the river water,

down large smears of red
that ran when we

paddled, the cluster
of willow

yellow where
the leaves fell.

In this slanty light

suspended, the canoe
stood still

on the water, the lovely

reflections not daring
to breathe,

the black surface of
water all dappled

with pollen. Though the dark

river ached
with its knowledge,

regrets; it
was not the day for them:

live on, live on.
We bent to the paddles.

Big headed, new born, the bunny is brought me;
how stubbornly it tries to stay alive
on its second day of life.

A field rabbit, dug from its nest by a dog,
his mother raked open, his littermates
laid in the cold and explored

by a curious paw
till their breath squeaked shut in protest:
now I am faced with this fuzzy survivor;

both eyes refusing, his small pink mouthgap
over the milktooth, clenching
and breathing hard. He's barely over an inch,

but already the twin ears wait for a signal,
the body barrel holds, the belly swells
daily, the tail flips up so I see

that a rabbit's tail is really
the fluffed underside of a normal tail
bending backwards. Feedings

go on. He responds,
feebly hopping a bit after each,
supporting that huge unintelligent head

on cramped haunches, quivering and weak,
and at three in the morning
the first eye opens.

And the next day the second. Dark,
disconcerting, does he now see?
But he sits in my hand still, too docile,

and his head grows larger. Luminous
and psychic, he recalls and broods on
his womb origins. He starts to tremble more,

and now he cannot stand. He will not
suck. He wobbles
in the warmth of the heating pad.

He looks backward; he looks forward
to the end of breathing:
he desires to be no longer form.

So briefly he has been the perfect
one of many, with mysterious
electric tangles that are eyes:

life, life in the shape of a rabbit!
Life, with your long ears!
I breathe on you, and try to fix what fades.

This morning, waking to the firm
dictum of water,
the house submitting like an invalid,
the mattress turning over and going back to sleep,

the oven brooding its load of bread,
things growing quietly in the cellar,
my hands clenched like roots,
I refuse the warm huddle and go out.

Locking eyes with the mist
the garden challenges,
sticks and stones pricking
up through the rain, steady, brown,

and macadam is shining. Excited,
the streets breathe rapidly.
Bird feathers, leaves
are cleared: the greedy drinking of gutters,

a thirst nailing the ground
into dark patterns.
Crosses, swastikas, no matter;
I am drawn to them, lulled, unjudging,

undergoing villages without a sign,
vast highways swishing
by, the hiss of wet car wheels,
the water wandering, the continental

divide. Strangers,
there is no name on my body;
the rain soothes like unanswerable
questions, the roads, toward some revelation,

overflow; the wanderer, urgent,
hurries through rivers.
Blood rises in waves in response to the wet;
the rich steam moist in the air,

the fields, loam and manure mixing,
exhaling under their blanket,
the chickens flurrying and niggling,
the grey boxes of band-aids, the cities:

the whole earth sliding in the downward
direction. Where do you run, roads,
lush with water? To what meeting
of cabalistic signs?—To the torrent;

to the unburdening. To the confessional
down by the ocean. The water foams there
like a leap of the heart: I spring
with the lake fish for land-locked release.